Counting on Pizza

Mick Gowar & Lesley Harker

W
FRANKLIN WATTS
LONDON • SYDNEY

It was Wednesday night and Mum
said, "I'm fed up with cooking.
I'm sick of slicing and chopping,
steaming and simmering.
So I'm not doing any of it tonight."
"But what about our tea?" we all asked.
"Easy!" said Mum. "We'll go and get
a pizza – and Dad can pay!"
And we all said, "YES!"

We all went in. "Right!" said Dad. "We'll have one family-sized cheese and tomato pizza—" "With pineapple," said Mum.

"Right!" said Dad. "We'll have one cheese and tomato pizza with two rings of pineapple—" "And peppers," said Jack.

1

2

"Right!" said Dad. "We'll have one cheese and tomato pizza with two pineapple rings, three peppers—"
"And pepperoni," I said.

"Right!" said Dad. "We'll have one cheese and tomato pizza with two rings of pineapple, three peppers, four slices of pepperoni—"

"And anchovies," said Mum.
"I love anchovies!"
"Right!" said Dad. "We'll have one
pizza with two rings of pineapple, three
peppers, four slices of pepperoni, five
anchovies—"
"And olives," said Jack.

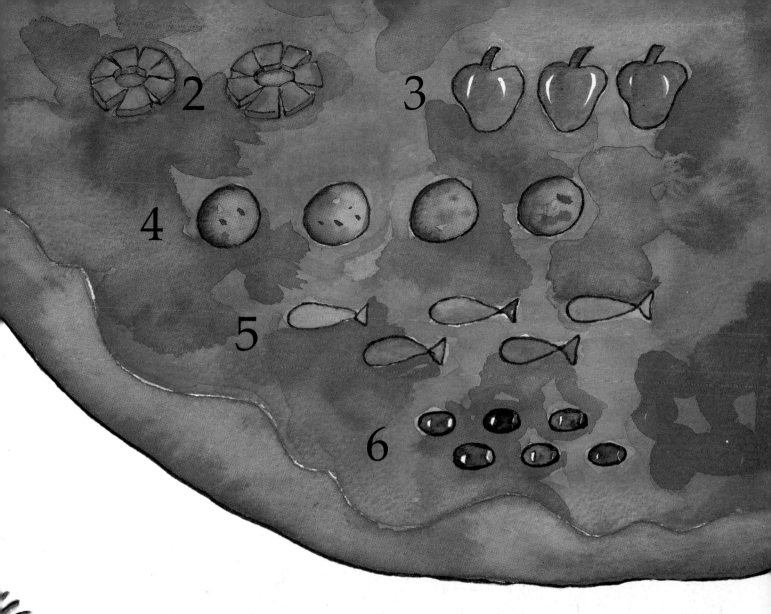

2

3

4

5

6

"Right!" said Dad. "We'll have one pizza with two rings of pineapple, three peppers, four slices of pepperoni, five anchovies, six olives—"

"And mushrooms!" I said.
"Right!" said Dad. "We'll
have pizza with two rings
of pineapple, three peppers,
four slices of pepperoni,
five anchovies, six olives,
seven mushrooms—"
"And ham," said Mum,
"to go with the pineapple."

"Right!" said Dad. "We'll have one pizza with two rings of pineapple, three peppers, four slices of pepperoni, five anchovies, six olives, seven mushrooms, eight pieces of ham—"

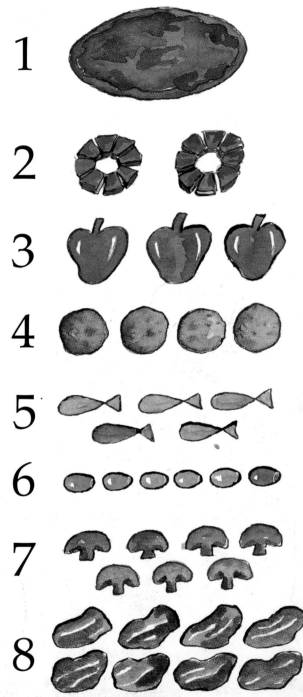

1

2

3

4

5

6

7

8

"And onion rings," said Jack. "Right!" said Dad. "We'll have one pizza with two pineapple rings, three peppers, four slices of pepperoni, five anchovies, six olives, seven mushrooms, eight pieces of ham, nine onion rings—"
"And sweetcorn," I said.
"To finish it off."

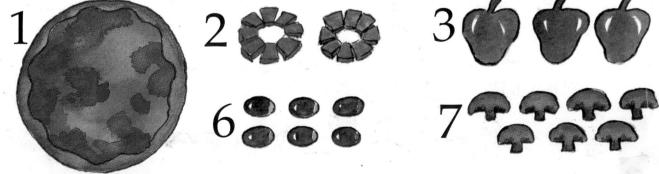

"Right!" said Dad. "We'll have one pizza with two pineapple rings, three peppers, four slices of pepperoni, five anchovies, six olives, seven mushrooms, eight pieces of ham, nine onion rings and ten bits of sweetcorn. And that's it!"

4 ● ● ● ●

5 🐟 🐟 🐟 🐟 🐟

9 ⭕ ⭕ ⭕ ⭕ ⭕ ⭕ ⭕ ⭕ ⭕

8 🍖 🍖 🍖 🍖 🍖 🍖 🍖 🍖

10 ◾ ◾ ◾ ◾ ◾ ◾ ◾ ◾ ◾ ◾

"Oh, no!" said Dad. "I left my wallet at home!" Mum emptied out her purse. Two pounds, three bus tickets, and a button.
"Oh dear," said Mum. "That's not enough." She thought for a moment, "There's only one thing we can do," she said.

"Please cancel the last order. We'll start again. We'll have one family-sized cheese and tomato pizza..."

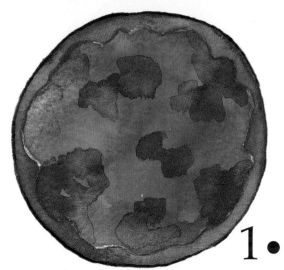

1• one

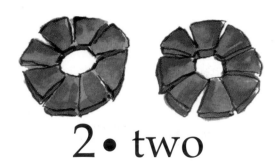

2• two

3• three

4• four

5• five

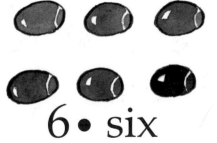

6• six

7 • seven

8 • eight

9 • nine

10 • ten

Sharing books with your child

Me and My World are a range of books for you to share with your child. Together you can look at the pictures and talk about the subject or story. Listening, looking and talking are the first vital stages in children's reading development, and lay the early foundation for good reading habits.

Talking about the pictures is the first step in involving children in the pages of a book, especially if the subject or story can be related to their own familiar world. When children can relate the matter in the book to their own experience, this can be used as a starting point for introducing new knowledge, whether it is counting, getting to know colours or finding out how other people live.

Gradually children will develop their listening and concentration skills as well as a sense of what a book is. Soon they will learn how a book works: that you turn the pages from right to left, and read the story from left to right on a double page. They start to realize that the black marks on the page have a meaning and that they relate to the pictures. Once children have grasped these basic essentials they will develop strategies for "decoding" the text such as matching words and pictures, and recognising the rhythm of the language in order to predict what comes next. Soon they will start to take on the role of an independent reader, handling and looking at books even if they can't yet read the words.

Most important of all, children should realize that books are a source of pleasure. This stems from your reading sessions which are times of mutual enjoyment and shared experience. It is then that children find the key to becoming real readers.

This edition 2003

Franklin Watts
96 Leonard Street,
London EC2A 4XD

Franklin Watts Australia
45-51 Huntley Street
Alexandria NSW 2015

ISBN 0 7496 4916 X

A CIP catalogue record for this book is available from the British Library

First published as *Jack and Me and the Pizza* in the Early Worms series

Printed in Belgium

Consultant advice: Sue Robson and Alison Kelly,
Senior Lecturers in Education,
Faculty of Education, Early Childhood Centre,
Roehampton Institute, London.